A FÖREVER HÖME FOR LUNA

LINDA CHAPMAN

Illustrated By
Sophy Williams

nosy crow

First published in the UK in 2020 by Nosy Crow Ltd
The Crow's Nest, 14 Baden Place
Crosby Row, London SE1 1YW

www.nosycrow.com

ISBN: 978 1 78800 945 4

A CIP catalogue record for this book will be available from the British Library.

Printed and bound in Great Britain by Clays Ltd, Elcograf S.p.A.

Papers used by Nosy Crow are made from
wood grown in sustainable forests.

MIX
Paper from
responsible sources
FSC® C018072

1 3 5 7 9 10 8 6 4 2

To Simba, the most loyal
and loving Golden Retriever in the world.

CHAPTER 1

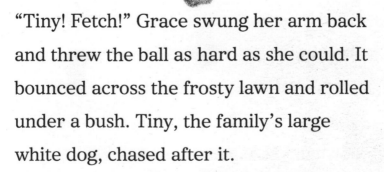

"Tiny! Fetch!" Grace swung her arm back
and threw the ball as hard as she could. It
bounced across the frosty lawn and rolled
under a bush. Tiny, the family's large
white dog, chased after it.

Jack, Grace's twin, laughed as Tiny

    1

scrabbled under the bush for the ball. His bottom was stuck up in the air, his fluffy tail wagging hard.

"Where's it gone, eh, Tiny?" Grace ran over to help as the dog wriggled further under the bush. She heard a loud hiss, then Tiny yelped and hurriedly backed out.

Jack came running. "What happened? Did he get stung?" he said, examining Tiny's face. The big dog was pawing at a little scratch on his nose.

Grace peered into the bush. "There's something in there." She knelt down and gently pulled the branches apart.

"Careful, it might be a snake," said Jack, squatting down next to Grace.

Grace gasped. "Oh, Jack! Look!" A tiny,

tortoiseshell kitten was crouching between the fallen leaves. It stared at Grace and Jack with wary blue eyes.

"It's so cute! I wonder where it's come from," said Jack.

Grace crawled closer. The ginger, black and white kitten shrank away at first but after a few moments it edged forwards

to sniff Grace's outstretched hand. Grace carefully caught hold of it.

"Ouch! Its claws are like pins," she said, backing out of the hedge. "I think it's scared of Tiny." The kitten wriggled and twisted in her hands. It seemed to be trying to climb on to the top of Grace's head.

"I'll put him in the house," said Jack.

"And I'll take the kitten to our shed.
Meet me there," said Grace.

Grace and Jack had a shed at the bottom
of the garden where they ran their animal
rehoming service, Forever Homes. The
nine-year-old twins made it their mission
to find any dog or cat the perfect owner,
and, until they did, the animal lived with
them.

As Jack took Tiny back to the house, the kitten relaxed into Grace's neck. "You're tickling me!" she giggled.

Grace entered the shed and let out a happy sigh as she looked at the photos on the walls of all the pets she and Jack had rehomed. Carefully, she stepped round the crate of cat and dog toys and sat on a bean bag with the kitten in her lap.

"You're so pretty!" Grace stroked the kitten's soft head. The little cat had tiny black ears that pointed straight up like a pixie's, a black and ginger face, and its tummy was like a half-moon of white fur. Its front paws were white and its tail was black and ginger. It purred as Grace stroked it.

"You like that, don't you?" Grace said. The kitten rubbed its face against Grace's hand.

Jack came in quietly, so as not to startle their little visitor. "Hello, puss-cat. What were you doing in our garden?" He stroked her too. "She must be a girl, mustn't she, because she's a tortoiseshell?"

Grace nodded. She and Jack knew a

lot about animals and both knew that tortoiseshell cats were nearly always female. "She's got an identity tag on." Grace found the fish-shaped name tag. "She's called Luna. That's cute. Do you want to hold her, Jack? She seems to love being cuddled."

"Hello, little pusskins," said Jack, taking Luna from his sister. He stroked her gently and checked the back of her tag. "It says she belongs to Susan Peters. That's Mum's friend! She only lives four doors up. We should take her home."

"Susan can't have had her for long," said Grace. "Luna is so tiny, she can't be much more than eight weeks old."

Jack reached into a cupboard. "I'll get the pet carrier, just in case we meet any

dogs on the way."

Luna didn't like the look of the pet
carrier. It took ages and lots of cat treats
before they managed to coax her inside.

"We'd better tell Mum where we're
going," said Grace as they walked towards
the neat-looking building where their
mother ran her doggy day care business,
Top Dog.

"Hello, you two." Mum smiled as they stamped their wellies on the mat. She looked in the pet carrier. "What have you got here? Another kitten to rehome? What a cutie!"

"She's not a Forever Homes kitten. She belongs to Susan Peters. We think she might have got lost," Grace explained. "We're about to take her home."

"Susan did say she was getting a new kitten," Mum said. "OK, take her back, but don't be long. Dad's cooking dinner."

Grace and Jack hurried along to Susan's house. As they crossed her frozen front garden, they saw Susan's other two cats watching them. One was a large tabby and the other was a fluffy tortoiseshell.

"They're checking us out," whispered

Grace as they waited for the front door to open.

Jack nodded. "They so are. The tabby hasn't even blinked yet."

The door opened and Susan Peters looked at Grace and Jack in surprise. "Hello, twins, is that a kitten? I hope you're not going to ask me to rehome it! I've only just got a new cat. My daughter bought her for me as a surprise. She meant well," she added with a sigh.

"Actually, this is your kitten," said Grace, holding out the carrier. "We found her in our garden."

"Oh, my goodness!" Susan peered into the carrier. The kitten mewed at her and Susan tickled her with one finger through the bars. "How did you escape from the garden, Luna?" She smiled at the twins. "Thanks for bringing her back. Please, do come in." As Susan stood back to let them into the hall the tabby and the tortoiseshell rushed past her. They charged upstairs together, knocking over a box of Christmas decorations on the bottom step. Grace felt Luna shrink into a corner of the pet carrier.

Susan sighed as she put the decorations back in the box. "Poor Luna. She's such a timid little thing. Teddy and Tabitha terrify her. They can get very boisterous when they play. I thought the garden was safe but I'd clearly better check the fence for gaps."

"How old is Luna?" asked Jack.

"Ten weeks. She's adorable but

I don't think this is the right home for her. She really needs to be the only cat."

Grace and Jack exchanged a look. It wasn't unusual for them to know what each other was thinking, but this time even Susan guessed too.

"Of course! Your pet rehoming business!" She looked at them. "Might you be able to find a new home and owner for her? Someone with no pets? I don't think it's fair to keep her here with my two terrors."

"Yes, we definitely can," said Grace and Jack together.

Susan smiled sadly. "I'll miss her but I think it might be for the best. Should I ring your mum first?"

"Mum will be fine," said Jack. "We're

not looking after any other animals at the
moment. We do need you to come round
to sign the paperwork, though. You have
to officially give Luna to us."

"Of course! I can do that now, if you like.
I'll just get Luna's things. She has a new
bed and you can have her bowls and toys.
Hopefully, it won't be too difficult to find a
lovely owner for her."

Grace peeped inside
the cat carrier.
Luna was hiding
right at the
back. "We're
going to find
you somewhere
quiet to live,
Luna."

"A home where there aren't any scary big cats," Jack agreed.

Grace grinned. She couldn't wait to start finding Luna the perfect new home!

CHAPTER 2

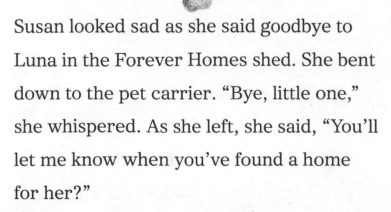

Susan looked sad as she said goodbye to Luna in the Forever Homes shed. She bent down to the pet carrier. "Bye, little one," she whispered. As she left, she said, "You'll let me know when you've found a home for her?"

    17

"Of course," said Grace and Jack together.

The little portable radiator that Mum had given the twins for the shed meant it was lovely and cosy, and last weekend they'd put up red and gold tinsel to make it look festive. Jack settled down to make some notes about the kitten in the Forever Homes notebook while Grace tried to coax Luna out of the pet carrier. Having not wanted to go in, the kitten now didn't want to come out again!

"Here, Luna." Grace held out a fish-shaped treat. The little cat's nose twitched but she stayed huddled at the back of the carrier.

Jack watched her. "Very timid," he said, writing in his book. "We already know

that Luna needs a quiet home where there aren't any cats or dogs. I guess that also rules out big families with lots of noisy children."

"She's coming out, Jack!" Grace whispered. She sat very still as Luna padded out of the pet carrier and stared round at her new surroundings. Jack watched quietly from the beanbag. After a bit, Luna was brave enough to start to explore. She walked around them and sniffed at Jack's foot. Jack's shoulders trembled as he tried not to laugh.

"Hello, little kitty." Grace reached out her hand. Luna rubbed against her fingers and purred.

Jack stroked Luna along her spine and the kitten arched her back. Jack grinned

and picked up his pen. "Loves attention,"
he wrote.

Attracted by his pen, Luna climbed into
his lap and began to knead his jeans with
her claws.

"Ow! Ow! Ow!" winced Jack. "I think she
likes me." He pushed the notebook away.
"Get one of her toys out, Grace. Let's see
if she's playful."

Grace pulled a mouse with a long tail out
of the bag of things that Susan had given
them and wiggled it in front of Luna.

The kitten jumped from Jack's lap and
pounced. Grace giggled and pulled the
mouse across the floor. Luna chased
after it. "OK, I think you can write down
that she loves to play!" said Grace. She
teased Luna with the mouse and the twins
laughed as the kitten darted about trying
to catch it.

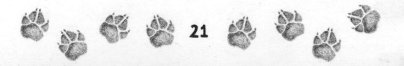

Suddenly, the door banged open. Cold air rushed into the shed as Amelia, the twins' thirteen-year-old sister came in. Luna hissed in shock. Her fur bristled and her tail stuck up in the air like a furry loo brush. She fled under the desk.

"Shut the door!" Grace gasped, worried in case Luna tried to escape.

Amelia frowned but shut the door behind her. "Dinner's nearly ready," she said.

"You have to come and lay the table."

"You frightened Luna!" said Jack crossly. "You should have knocked first, not just barged in."

Amelia raised her eyebrows. "Maybe next time I won't bother telling you dinner's ready. Who's Luna, anyway?"

Grace crawled under the desk, then backed out slowly with Luna in her hands. The tiny kitten stared up at Amelia with wide eyes.

Amelia's grumpy mood melted away as she saw the cute kitten. "Awww, she's gorgeous. Doesn't she like people, though? Why's she so scared?"

"She's really shy," said Grace. "You can stroke her if you want."

"But gently," warned Jack.

"Durrr, I'm not stupid," said Amelia, pulling a face at him, but as she turned to Luna, her voice softened. "Hey, little kitten, do you want to come to your Auntie Amelia for a cuddle?" She tickled Luna under the chin and the kitten allowed herself to be handed over. Amelia held her close. Both she and Ollie, the twins' older brother, loved animals, even if they weren't quite as animal-mad as the twins.

"We need to find her a home with no other animals and no young children," said Jack.

"I'll ask around," said Amelia. "All my friends are obsessed with cute cat videos."

"Oh!" said Grace. "That gives me an idea. Ms Drew was looking at pictures of kittens on her phone when we had wet

play last week. Maybe she'd like to adopt a cat? She seems like a quiet person."

"Good idea," said Jack. "She's really nice. Let's ask her tomorrow!"

The following morning, Grace and Jack arrived in school early and went straight to their classroom. Their teacher, Ms Drew, was marking books at her desk.

"Hello, twins," she said with a smile. "You're early today. How can I help you?"

Grace explained while Jack pulled a photo of Luna from his bag and showed it to Ms Drew.

"She looks gorgeous," said Ms Drew. "But you're too late, I'm afraid. I went to see a litter of kittens just a few days ago and chose one. I'm so sorry. Much as I'd like two cats, I really don't think I can manage it."

"It's OK, miss," said Jack with a sigh. "Luna needs to go to a home where she's the only cat anyway."

"I promise if I hear of anyone else who wants a kitten I'll let you know," said their teacher.

Grace and Jack nodded and went outside to join their friends, who were running round in the playground to keep warm.

Chloe was sliding across the icy ground as if it was an ice rink. She had only joined the class a few months ago but she and the twins got on brilliantly.

"Guess what?" she said. "I'm going to go to that new theme park on Saturday, the one with the Monster ride. It's a triple

   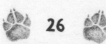

loop helter-skelter." Words seemed to rush out of Chloe. Her curly hair was sticking out in all directions and, as always, she couldn't seem to stand still. "My mum's godson, Freddie, is coming too. He's eight. His parents have to work and he doesn't have any brothers or sisters to play with so he gets he's lonely. I haven't seen him for ages. I hope he'll go on the Monster with me! We're going to ask your mum if she can look after Tilly so she's not on her own all day." She grinned. "I bet Tilly would love to go on a helter-skelter if she was allowed!"

Tilly was a cheeky cockapoo with wavy cream fur that the twins had rehomed with Chloe a while ago.

"Wow! Lucky you! Ollie's taking me and

Grace to the theme park but not until the summer," said Jack.

"I wish I was going this weekend. I can't wait to go on the Monster," said Grace.

"I like the teacups best," said Jack.

"Boring!" said Grace.

Chloe giggled. "I love all the rides but I hate going to theme parks on my own. It's going to be fun having Freddie with me."

Just then the bell rang and the children ran to start the line for their class.

The rest of the day went by quickly. Grace and Jack hurried home, eager to check on Luna. As they burst into the kitchen, they saw Ollie, their seventeen-year-old brother, standing by the curtains. He swung round when he heard them, his eyes widening guiltily. He spread his arms.

   28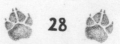

"What are you hiding?"
Jack demanded.

"Nothing," Ollie said quickly.

"You so are." Grace lunged
and prodded him in the
tummy

"Oof!" gasped Ollie,
doubling over. The
twins saw Luna clinging
to the curtain, halfway
up, her eyes wide and
her whiskers trembling.
"I didn't mean to frighten
her," Ollie said quickly. "I got this
great idea for a tune and I was
drumming it out on the table. I
didn't know Luna was under there
until she ran up the curtain!"

"Oh, Ollie!" groaned Grace. "Help me, Jack. I think she's got a claw stuck."

"Poor little Luna," Jack soothed, while Grace stood on a chair and unhooked Luna's claw. When Luna was free, Grace lifted her down.

"No drumming until we've found Luna a new home." Grace gave Ollie a hard stare. "Promise?"

"I promise!" said Ollie meekly. He reached out and stroked Luna. "I didn't mean to frighten her. This house is pretty noisy. I hope you find a new home for her soon, where she'll have peace and quiet."

"We do too," said Jack, stroking Luna's soft head.

 30

CHAPTER 3

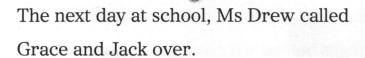

The next day at school, Ms Drew called Grace and Jack over.

"Have you found a home for your kitten yet?" she asked. The twins shook their heads. "Oh good! My friend Helen's looking for a cat."

     31

"Luna's very timid and needs a quiet environment," said Jack, wishing he had his notebook so he could interview Ms Drew properly. "Could your friend provide such a home?"

Ms Drew hid a smile. "Well, Helen lives with her elderly father and there are no young children or pets in the house."

"That sounds perfect!" said Grace.

Jack frowned at his sister. He wished she'd remember they had to do things properly. "Your friend and her father will need to pass our Forever Home checks before we can say for sure," said Jack seriously. "And we will have to do a home visit in order to make a proper assessment."

He took a card from his school bag.

On it was the Forever Homes paw print drawn in sparkly gel pen and their phone number.

"Thanks," said Ms Drew. "I'll give it to Helen and hopefully she'll get in touch."

"Thanks, miss!" said Grace, as Jack nodded in approval.

The twins went to sit down. "Helen sounds perfect for Luna!" said Grace in excitement.

Jack tutted. "She might be, and I hope so too, but we won't know until we meet her and do a home visit."

Grace crossed her fingers tightly. She fell in love with every single pet they rehomed. It was always hard to let them go but at the same time she knew they couldn't keep them all. It would be

brilliant if Ms Drew's friend could give
Luna her Forever Home.

After school, the twins got a call from
Helen. She asked if she could come around
to see Luna that evening.

"Can she, Mum?" asked Grace, covering
the phone with her hand.

"Of course," Mum replied. "But you'd
better tidy the kitchen up first."

By the time Helen arrived, the twins had
cleared the kitchen and put Luna in her
carrier to keep her safe.

Grace liked Helen immediately. She was
quietly spoken and didn't poke her finger
through the bars of the pet carrier at
Luna.

"She's such a pretty colour! Do you

think she might let me stroke her?" asked
Helen.

"I'm sure she will," said Jack, smiling.
"Why don't you sit down first?"

Grace felt her heart lift. She could tell
her brother liked Helen too.

Luna seemed
happy to be put
in Helen's lap.
Grace stood
back, crossing
her fingers.

Luna's blue
eyes were
huge as she
looked around,
but as the twins began
Helen's interview, Luna relaxed. She

kneaded Helen's leg, turned in a circle then sat down. Helen stroked her head and before long Luna began to purr.

Grace exchanged a delighted look with Jack. This was looking really good! Helen had told them she owned a house with

a garden in a quiet cul-de-sac with very little traffic. She worked part time and lived with her father, who was happy to look after a cat when Helen was out or away. Most importantly Luna seemed to like Helen. Her purrs were getting louder as Helen stroked her.

"We'd need to do a home check but you seem like you might be perfect," said Jack at last.

Helen beamed. "That's great. Are your parents free to bring you to mine now – Luna too? You could do the home check and then, if I pass, she can stay. I've got cat bowls and I can get some food from the corner shop."

Jack went to find Mum. She was busy with paperwork but Ollie offered to drive the twins and Luna to Helen's house. Grace could hardly sit still in the car as they followed Helen home.

Jack glanced at her. "Don't get too excited yet," he warned. "Helen might have forgotten to tell us that there's a train line at the bottom of her garden or something."

Grace rolled her eyes. "Don't be silly, Jack. This is going to be the perfect home for Luna, I just know it!"

   38

CHAPTER 4

Ollie parked the car outside Helen's house. The front garden was neat and tidy with lots of bushes for Luna to hide under. Inside, the house was small but cosy.

"You can let Luna out in the kitchen while I get my dad," said Helen, pointing along the hall. She knocked on a door by the stairs. "Dad, are you there?"

Grace led the way. "It's nice here," she whispered, putting the carrier on the kitchen floor.

Jack nodded. "She's already got a cat flap," he said, looking at the back door.

"Stand still, Ollie," warned Grace as she opened the carrier. Luna emerged slowly, her tail twitching as she took in her new surroundings.

"So you're the Forever Twins," boomed a voice.

Luna jumped and the twins spun round, blinking in surprise at the large man standing in the doorway. He looked just like Father Christmas with his huge belly and bushy white beard!

"I'm Jack and this is my sister Grace," said Jack politely. "We're from Forever Homes."

"I'm Jack, too!" said the old man. "Big Jack. All the best people are Jacks! So this is the kitten?" He burst into song. "*Oh, Luna! Luna, my love!*" As he sang, he threw out his arms and knocked a spoon off the table. It clattered loudly on the tiled

floor. Big Jack roared with laughter.

Luna dived back inside the cat carrier.

"Dad! You've frightened her," said Helen, following him into the room. "It's all right, poppet, he's not going to hurt you." Helen crouched down and after some gentle persuading, the kitten let Helen lift her out.

"Look at her, she's nothing but a tiny wee scrap!" boomed Big Jack. He moved towards Luna but trod on the spoon, tripped and stumbled.

Luna let out a meow. Clawing her way up Helen she tried to hide behind her hair.

"Ouch!" Helen gently untangled the kitten. "You'd better go, Dad. You're scaring her. I'll pop in to see you in a bit."

Once Big Jack had left, Luna relaxed and

let Helen cuddle her.

But Helen looked at the twins sadly. "Dad's not the quietest of people, as you can see. I'd love to take Luna but having seen how nervous she is, I don't think I could give her the right home after all. Not unless you can find a new Forever Home for Dad!"

Ollie grinned. "Sorry but they only take in cats and dogs."

"Probably just as well!" Helen sighed and gave the kitten a big cuddle. "I'm so sorry."

"That's OK," said Grace, hiding her disappointment. "Thanks for letting us visit."

The twins put Luna back in her carrier and Ollie drove them all home again.

By Saturday morning, Grace and Jack had only had one other enquiry about Luna, from a man who already had a cat.

"He didn't read the poster properly," said Grace when she came off the phone.

Chloe came round to drop Tilly off on her way to the theme park.
The cream cockapoo
went wild when
she saw

Grace and Jack and their mum. She jumped round their legs and yelped with excitement.

"Freddie's waiting in the van with Mum," said Chloe. "He saw Tiny in the garden and wouldn't come in with me. He doesn't like dogs much. Not even Tilly." She pulled a face. "He's not as much fun as I remembered." She handed Tilly's lead to the twins' mum. "Thanks, Mrs Taylor. I need to get a move on. There's always a queue to ride the Monster and I want at least two goes!"

Mrs Taylor laughed. "I hope you've got a warm coat then. It's getting colder. Take as long as you like at the park. Tilly's a special client and I'll keep her for as long as you need."

'Thanks, Mrs T. You're the best! Monster roller coaster, here I come!" Chloe waved and hurtled back to the car.

CHAPTER 5

Grace opened the kitchen door. "It's so warm in here!" She and Jack had just come back from taking Tilly and Tiny on their afternoon walk to the park.

"I wonder if Chloe's having fun," Grace continued, flinging off her hat and scarf.

"I bet she is! I wish I'd been at the theme park today."

"But it's been lovely looking after Tilly," said Jack, following her inside. "I'd rather play with her than go on a roller coaster."

"I'd like to do both!" said Grace with a grin. "Shut the door, Jack. It's so cold. I hope it's going to snow some more."

"Wait up!" said a voice. They turned and saw Chloe opening the gate.

"You're back early," said Jack in surprise.

"How was the Monster?" asked Grace eagerly.

Chloe crouched down as Tilly ran over to greet her. She pulled a face. "Not fun. I had to sit next to some old person cos Freddie wouldn't come on it with me."

    48

"Bad luck," said Jack. "Why didn't he go on it?"

"He's scared of heights," Chloe groaned. "He wouldn't go on anything except for the merry-go-round. Four times on a unicorn. How lame is that? Then he said he was cold. That's why we're back so early. He's so boring."

    49

"Oh, dear," said Mrs Taylor, walking over from the Top Dog building. "Why not ask your mum to come in for a cup of tea and you and Freddie can play with the twins for a bit?"

Chloe beamed. "Thanks, Mrs T. I'll go and tell them." She shoved Tilly's lead at her and ran off.

"I'll put the kettle on," Mum said. "Jack, you'd best put Tiny and Tilly in the lounge if Freddie doesn't like dogs."

Chloe came back with her mum and Freddie. Grace looked at the boy curiously. He was small and skinny, with an anxious expression, and stood stiffly, half hiding behind Chloe's mum until the two women went into the lounge to chat.

Grace and Jack got out some crisps and

juice to share with Freddie and Chloe.

Looking round, Grace realised Freddie had crawled under the kitchen table. He was holding out his hand, making soft noises at Luna. Luna stared at him with unblinking eyes. Grace watched curiously. Would the kitten run away? To her surprise, Luna stepped forward to rub her head against Freddie's hand.

A smile spread across Freddie's face.

Grace nudged Jack and pointed under the table. Luna was stepping on to Freddie's knee and Freddie was watching her intently.

Chloe rolled her eyes at the twins. "Weird!" she mouthed.

"Are you OK, Freddie?" Jack asked, peering under the table. "Do you want some crisps?"

Freddie shook his head. "Can I stay with the kitten? I love cats. I really, *really* want one but Mum and Dad haven't said yes yet."

Grace and Jack looked at each other. Could Freddie be a new owner for Luna?

"Jack, why don't you and Chloe go outside and play football?" suggested

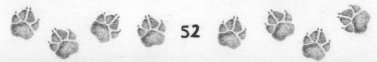

Grace. "I'll join you in a minute."

"Yes, let's go!" said Chloe, leaping up. "Come on, Tilly! Come on, Jack!"

Chloe yanked the door open. "It's snowing!" she cried, running outside. Jack gave Grace an encouraging nod and then followed Chloe, closing the door behind him.

Grace pretended to be looking for her shoes, while secretly she watched Freddie. He seemed a lot like Luna – cautious and nervous. Grace felt she had to be careful not to startle him. She got the crisps and crouched down. "Do you want to come out and have some crisps?"

"Um..." He looked tempted but kept stroking Luna, who was now curled up on his knee. "It's OK. I'll stay here. I don't want to move your kitten."

"Don't worry," said Grace. "She won't mind if you carry her out."

Freddie hesitated and then gathered Luna in his arms and edged out on his bottom. He settled with his back to a table leg and Luna curled up on his lap again. He stroked her with one hand and took some crisps with the other. He smiled shyly at Grace.

She munched on her crisps. "So, you want a cat?" she said conversationally.

"Oh, yes," muttered Freddie, staring down at Luna. "You're so lucky to have one. Mum and Dad both work really hard and it's lonely when they're working and I've got no one to play with."

"Have you got room for a kitten?" Grace

waited eagerly for his reply.

"I've been reading lots of cat books and our house is perfect. We've got a big garden and we live on a very quiet lane with hardly any traffic. And I read all about what to feed them and how to take care of them." Freddie's face clouded over. "I know a kitten would be happy with us but Mum and Dad say they haven't got time to go searching for a pet." He sighed, and looked earnestly at Grace. "I want a cat more than I want anything else in the world. I'd like one just like Luna."

Grace couldn't hold herself back any more. "Listen, Freddie, if we can persuade your parents then maybe you could have—"

The back door flew open with a bang and

Chloe came hurtling in. "Mum! Mum! I slipped over! I need a plaster!"

Luna jumped as the door banged, her claws tightening on Freddie's legs.

"Ow!" shrieked Freddie. "That hurts!"

Luna leapt off his knee in alarm. Freddie rolled up his trouser leg and looked at the little scratch Luna had made. "I'm bleeding."

"Me, too!" said Chloe cheerfully. Gleefully, she pointed to a big graze on the

palm of one of her hands. "Look at all the blood!"

Grace's mum handed Chloe a tissue. "Sit down, Chloe. I'll get some wipes and a plaster and we can clean you up. And you, Freddie."

"Luna didn't mean to scratch you, Freddie," said Grace quickly. "She got frightened. Think how scary it must be for tiny Luna in a room full of noisy people. We must all seem like giants to her."

Freddie giggled. "I suppose." He looked round. "Where *is* Luna?"

The children searched the kitchen but the kitten was nowhere to be found.

"She must have gone outside," said Grace, grabbing her coat and running into the garden.

Jack was in the garden, making snowballs. The snow was falling heavily now, the thick flakes settling on the ground in a white carpet. He looked up in surprise as they all hurried out.

"We've lost Luna!" Grace cried. The icy air bit into her cheeks as she pulled her coat on. It was so cold out here. She

looked round desperately. Poor little Luna
– she'd freeze!

"Oh no!" she said in dismay. "The garden
gate's open!"

"Look! There are paw prints!" Jack ran
over to a trail of tiny prints in the snow.

"Everyone split up and search!" said Mrs
Taylor.

They spread out into the large garden. It
was getting dark and it wasn't easy to see
through the whirl of snowflakes.

"Luna!" called Grace, her voice muffled by the falling snow.

"Luna!" Chloe yelled.

"She's got to be here somewhere," said Freddie anxiously, peering under the snowy branches of a bush.

"Listen," said Jack suddenly. They all stood still. Then Grace heard it, too. A high-pitched mew, coming from a nearby oak tree.

"It's Luna!" cried Grace. "She's stuck up that tree!"

CHAPTER 6

Luna was high up the tree, her body flattened against the trunk as she clung on with her sharp claws. She was covered in snowflakes and looked terrified.

"Oh, poor kitten!" said Mum.

"It's my fault!" said Freddie, blinking

away tears. "I shouted and scared her. I'm so, so sorry."

Grace saw the guilt in his eyes. "You didn't mean to scare her. You only yelled because she scratched you."

"What are we going to do?" said Jack.

"We need a ladder," said Mum. "I'll go next door and see if we can borrow theirs."

"That will take ages!" said Freddie. "I'll climb up and get her." To Grace's surprise, he grabbed the lowest branch and began to climb the oak tree.

"Freddie, please stop, sweetie!" Chloe's mum called anxiously. "Let us get a ladder."

"No, I'm getting her," said Freddie stubbornly, pulling himself further up

the tree. "She trusts me!"

"But, Freddie, you hate heights!" protested Chloe. "Let me go instead. I'm much better at climbing! I'll rescue Luna!" She jigged from foot to foot. "Freddie!" she said loudly. "Come down!"

"Shhh!" he said sharply. "You'll scare her!"

Chloe's mouth dropped open in astonishment.

Freddie climbed higher and

higher. He was out of their reach now
and they had no way of stopping him.
Snowflakes swirled around them as they
watched anxiously. No one dared breathe
as he inched towards Luna. Finally, she
was within reach! He hesitated. How could
he pick the kitten up safely and still hang
on to the tree?

Grace knew what to do. "Pick her up by
the scruff of her neck," she shouted.

"I can't! It'll hurt her!" gasped Freddie,
his face pale.

"It won't," called Jack. "It's how mother
cats carry their kittens. There's extra skin
at the back of their necks so it doesn't
hurt. It'll be OK."

As Freddie hesitated, Luna started to
climb higher. In a flash, Freddie shot out

his arm and grabbed the back of her neck.
He pulled her away from the trunk. For a
heart-stopping moment the kitten dangled
in mid-air, then Freddie hugged her to his
chest.

The breath rushed out of Grace. For a
moment, she'd thought Luna was going to
fall.

"I've got her!" Freddie gasped.

"Well done!" Mum exclaimed.

Freddie tucked Luna inside his coat and
then slowly began to climb back down.
Near the bottom, he half slid, half jumped
from the tree.

Everyone surrounded him as he opened
his coat a little and took Luna out. He
gently rubbed his cheek against her fur as
she nuzzled against him.

    65

"Wow! That was amazing, Freddie!"
Chloe stared at her cousin with respect.

"Oh, Freddie!" said Chloe's mum.
"That was very brave but please don't do
anything like that ever again!"

Freddie turned pink.
"It wasn't brave. I
didn't go that high."

"You did!" said
Grace.

"You were brilliant!"
said Jack.

Freddie looked
down at the kitten in
his arms. "I'm sorry,
Luna," he said softly.

"You didn't mean to scratch me and I
shouldn't have yelled." He took a breath

and then offered her to Grace. "Here, you can have your kitten back."

"But she's not my kitten!" Grace knew she should talk to Jack first but the words were already tumbling out. "Jack and I are looking for a home for Luna. If we can persuade your parents, would you like her for your own?"

Freddie stared at Grace, his eyes as wide as Luna's. "She could be mine?" he faltered. "My very own?"

"Well, we'd have to do some house checks," Jack said quickly. "Fill in the right forms." Grace glanced at him but to her relief he didn't look that cross with her. "But if your house is suitable and your parents agree, then yes, she could be yours."

"Oh, wow." Freddie stared down at Luna as if he couldn't believe what he was hearing. Luna snuggled closer, rubbing the top of her head under his chin. "She's like my dream kitten – the kitten I'd always imagined having."

Luna purred.

Grace and Jack exchanged delighted looks and then glanced at mum, who was smiling at Freddie. "This seems to be working out very nicely," she said. "Now, why don't we go inside and get warm. Then we can ring your mum and dad and see what they say, Freddie."

CHAPTER 7

Jack got his notebook and ran through his questions one by one: what was Freddie's house like? Did it have a garden? Was there a busy road nearby? Was the house quiet?

Freddie answered all the questions

solemnly. "Our house is in the middle of nowhere. There's just me and my mum and dad. No pets. No brothers or sisters. I'd love a cat to keep me company. Mum and Dad are often busy with their work and I get lonely. I've read lots of cat books.

I know how to feed Luna properly. I know to take her to the vet for her check-ups. And I'd play with her."

"I'm sure Freddie would be an excellent pet owner," said Chloe's mum.

Freddie looked at Grace and Jack hopefully. "Do I pass? Can I have her?"

They swapped looks and nodded at the same time.

"Yes!" Grace told Freddie. "On this one occasion we can let you be Luna's new owner even though we can't do an actual visit. Your house sounds perfect."

"But your mum and dad have to say yes," Jack put in quickly.

"Let's ring Auntie Jane right now, Mum!" said Chloe, picking up her mother's phone and pressing some buttons.

    71

"Chloe—!" her mum protested, reaching for her mobile.

"Hi, Auntie Jane!" Chloe sang as her aunt answered. "You'll never guess what! Freddie's found a kitten he wants, to stop him being lonely. Yes, a kitten! At Forever Homes! It's soooooo cute!" Chloe was talking even faster than normal.

Grace and Jack swapped looks and held up their crossed fingers. Freddie cuddled Luna anxiously.

"Auntie Jane wants to speak to you," said Chloe at last, handing the phone to her mum.

Her mum explained a bit more about
what had been going on. "I know it's
sudden but she's a lovely kitten and she
does need a good home. She got into a
spot of bother in the garden and Freddie
was marvellous. He's very responsible
for his age and I'm sure he'd look after
her well. If you are thinking of getting
him a cat any time soon, then this might
be perfect timing. Yes... I see... I know... I
see..."

Grace's heart thudded as Freddie's face
grew more and more anxious. *Oh please,
say he can have Luna*, she thought. *Please!*

"OK, I'll tell him," said Chloe's mum. She
ended the call and turned to Freddie.

Grace saw Freddie's face pale. "Did
Mum say no?" he whispered.

Chloe's mum grinned. "She said yes! You can have Luna for your very own!"

Freddie's mouth fell open. "Your mum and dad are already on their way pick you up. They came early because of the snow. I've asked them to come straight here. I hope that was OK?"

Grace and Jack beamed. "Of course!" they chorused.

A little while later, when everyone was drinking steaming mugs of hot chocolate, a large car pulled up outside the house. Freddie carefully put Luna on the wide window ledge and ran to the kitchen door.

His mum and dad were stamping snow off their shoes on the doorstep. "Hi, Mum, hi, Dad, come in but don't make too much

noise. Luna is a bit timid."

He went back over to Luna, stretched out on the windowsill. When she saw who it was, she miaowed. He gently picked her up and she nestled into his arms, purring.

Freddie's dad was tall and thin, his mum round and plump with dark hair. Her face softened as soon as she saw Luna. "Oh,

what a gorgeous kitten. She's so pretty, Freddie."

"Hello, little kitten," said Freddie's dad, stroking Luna's head with one finger. He had a deep, rumbling voice but he spoke quietly to Luna. "I hear you're a bit timid? Well, we'll be very calm and quiet I'm sure you'll soon get used to us."

"Does that mean I can have her?" asked Freddie eagerly.

"I have a feeling we won't get you home without her," chuckled his mum. "Yes, she's yours if you want her. Your not-just-for-Christmas Christmas present!"

"Oh, wow," breathed Freddie. He hugged Luna. "You're coming home with me." He kissed the kitten's head and looked up with shining eyes. "This is the

happiest day of my life!"

Luna purred and nuzzled his hand.

Grace felt a rush of satisfaction as she looked at the two of them together. She was a hundred per cent sure that the little kitten really had found the perfect home!

Freddie's parents signed all the paperwork. The twins gave them some cat food and Luna's toys and basket and said they could borrow the cat carrier to take her home. They both gave Luna one last cuddle and then stood on the street and waved goodbye as Freddie's family drove off behind Chloe and her mum.

Freddie turned and waved out of the back window, the biggest smile on his face.

"We did it," Grace said, linking arms with Jack. "We found Luna a perfect new home. I think Freddie needs her as much as she needs him. I love a happy ending."

"Me too," said Jack. "And I think Luna's definitely going to get one with Freddie!"

"I wonder what animal will need our help next," said Grace. "Another kitten? A puppy? A dog or a cat?"

"A pet pig? A pony? An orangutan?" said Jack with a grin.

Grace chuckled. "Whatever it is – bring it on!"

OLLIE TAYLOR'S FACT FILE

NAME: Oliver Max Taylor

AGE: Seventeen

LIKES: Music, playing the drums, dogs, hanging out with mates

DISLIKES: Cold weather, wearing smart clothes

FAVOURITE COLOUR: Red

FAVOURITE FOODS: Burritos, chicken korma

FAVOURITE JOKE:

Q: What do you call a cow that can play a musical instrument?

A: A moo-sician

DREAM JOB: Being in a mega-famous band

WHAT ANIMAL WOULD YOU BE? A wolf, for their incredible looks and spine-tingling howl

HOW IS YOUR FELINE FEELING?

How good are you at understanding your cat? Answer these questions to find out!

1. YOUR **CAT** IS CROUCHING DOWN CLOSE TO THE FLOOR, ITS TAIL IS STILL, ITS EYES ARE WIDE AND ITS EARS ARE FLAT AGAINST ITS HEAD. IS IT:
    a) Happy
    b) Frightened
    c) Confident
    d) Angry

2. YOUR **CAT'S** FUR IS RAISED, ITS TAIL IS FLUFFED UP, IT'S HISSING, ITS EARS ARE POINTING TO THE SIDE AND ITS EYES ARE NARROWED. IS IT:

a) Happy

b) Frightened

c) Confident

d) Angry

3. YOUR CAT'S EYES ARE WIDE, ITS TAIL IS STRAIGHT UP, ITS FUR IS FLAT, ITS EARS ARE PRICKED AND POINTING FORWARD AND IT'S WALKING TOWARDS YOU. IS IT:

a) Happy

b) Frightened

c) Confident

d) Angry

4. **YOUR CAT IS SITTING ON YOUR LAP, ITS FUR IS SMOOTH, IT'S PURRING AND ITS EYES ARE HALF CLOSED. IS IT:**

a) Happy

b) Frightened

c) Confident

d) Angry

ANSWERS ON PAGE 89

GRACE AND JACK'S CLAW-SOME CAT JOKES!

WHERE DO YOU FIND A PRESENT FOR A CAT?

In a cat-alogue!

WHAT COLOUR DO CATS LIKE BEST?

Purr-ple!

WHY DID THE CAT RUN AWAY FROM THE TREE?

Because its bark scared her!

WHAT DO CATS LIKE FOR BREAKFAST?

Mice Krispies!

WHO BRINGS CATS PRESENTS AT CHRISTMAS?

Santa-Claws!

ANSWERS TO QUIZ ON PAGE 83-86

Answers: 1b, 2d, 3c, 4a